MW00965697

Screech Owl at Midnight Hollow

SMITHSONIAN'S BACKYARD

To Ellery Rose,
whose first word was "owl." — D.L.

To Joy — J.S.

Book Design: Shields & Partners, Westport, CT

First Edition 1996
10 9 8 7 6 5 4
Printed in China

Acknowledgements:
  Our very special thanks to Dr. Gary Graves of the Division of Birds at the Smithsonian's National Museum of Natural History for his curatorial review.

Screech Owl at Midnight Hollow

by C. Drew Lamm
Illustrated by Joel Snyder

Soundprints
Where Children Discover Nature

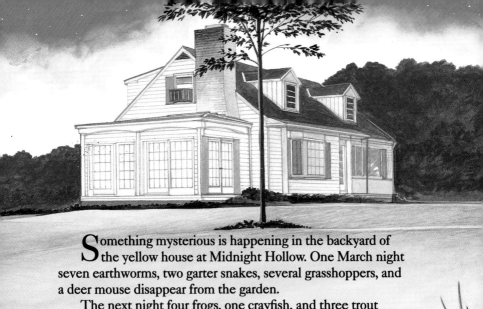

Something mysterious is happening in the backyard of
the yellow house at Midnight Hollow. One March night
seven earthworms, two garter snakes, several grasshoppers, and
a deer mouse disappear from the garden.

The next night four frogs, one crayfish, and three trout
disappear from the stream. By the fifth day seven song birds,
fourteen beetles, twenty-two moths, a dozen grasshoppers, six
crickets, and five meadow voles have all vanished.

There are other clues. Noises! Deep night noises.
First there were peeps. Then there were squeaks. Then
wild chatters followed by hums.

Two owls sit stone still in a sycamore tree above the
stream. Beside them, in a cavity made by a flicker, huddle
their five noisy nestlings — the noise makers.

During the day Mother and Father Screech Owl look like the bark. When a cat stalks the yard, they close their yellow eyes, stretch tall and thin, and blend in with the tree. They sleep waiting for the sun to set.

Once the sun sails under the horizon, once the back porch light clicks on, Mother and Father Screech Owl begin to stir.

As night falls, a quivering trill weaves through the trees. It slides down, down from the sycamore tree. Mice shiver with fright.

Father Screech Owl floats to the garden on silent wings. On rainy nights he stalks through puddles sucking up worms.

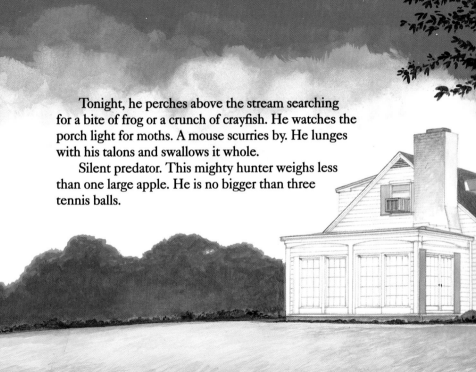

Tonight, he perches above the stream searching for a bite of frog or a crunch of crayfish. He watches the porch light for moths. A mouse scurries by. He lunges with his talons and swallows it whole.

Silent predator. This mighty hunter weighs less than one large apple. He is no bigger than three tennis balls.

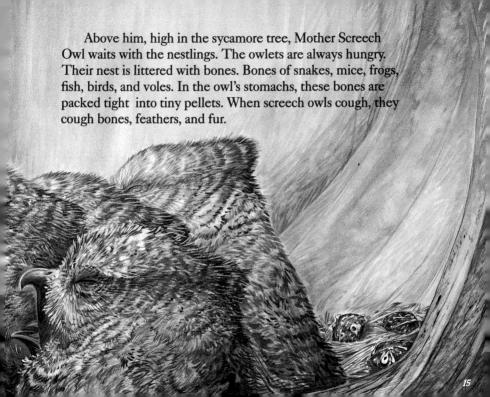

Above him, high in the sycamore tree, Mother Screech Owl waits with the nestlings. The owlets are always hungry. Their nest is littered with bones. Bones of snakes, mice, frogs, fish, birds, and voles. In the owl's stomachs, these bones are packed tight into tiny pellets. When screech owls cough, they cough bones, feathers, and fur.

Father returns home with fresh piles of moths, spiders, mice, and frogs. Mother tears off pieces and feeds these bites to the nestlings.

In between feedings she bathes in the backyard birdbath while Father Screech Owl watches over the nestlings.

On the sixth day the owlets start shivering. The nest is all shivers. And then the yawning begins. First one yawns, then another and another. Shivers and yawns.

In a little over a week they are covered by a new coat of feathers. They stop shivering. And they stop their crazy yawns. But their mouths are still wide open, begging for food.

By the end of the third week, their eyes are open —
a nest of lemon moons. Yellow moons blinking and wide
mouths waiting for mice.

By the fourth week they scramble out of the tree. They sit side by side on a branch. Parents drop whole mice into their gaping mouths.

A few nights later the largest owlet tries her first flight. The owlet teeters on the branch and then plummets to the ground. She scrambles to her toes. She digs her talons into the tree bark and skitters back up to the branch, more like a cat than an owl.

Her fluttering catches the attention of a great
horned owl. She'd be easy to pluck from the sycamore
branch — a delicious dinner. He aims for her. A twig pops as
he pushes off from the branch.

Mother Screech Owl snaps her head around. She catches
his flight with her sharp eyes. She hurls towards him. He veers
for her instead. Mother Screech Owl catapults away from the
sycamore tree, away from her baby owlet. The large owl plunges
straight for her.

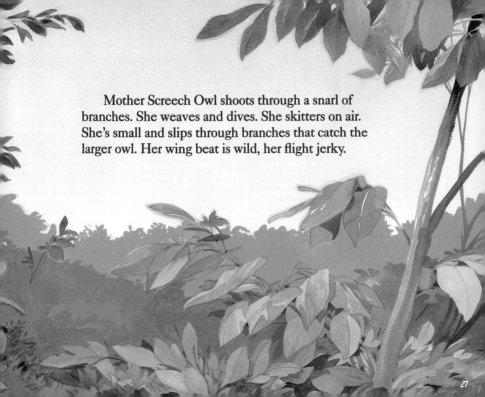

Mother Screech Owl shoots through a snarl of branches. She weaves and dives. She skitters on air. She's small and slips through branches that catch the larger owl. Her wing beat is wild, her flight jerky.

Branches slap the great horned owl as he flies after
Mother Screech Owl. Wind from his wings ripples her feathers.
Talons slice through the air.

The night is silent.

Then a triumphant trill slides down through the trees behind the yellow house. Up in the sycamore tree fourteen lemon moons blink. The screech owl family is safe — for tonight. The great horned owl flies home hungry.

Mother and Father Screech Owl stretch. Another owlet tries his first flight. One night soon, all of the owlets will fly. And they will snatch their own mice from the backyards of Midnight Hollow.

About the Screech Owl

Screech owls are found throughout the continental United States. They are nocturnal hunters, restricting most of their activity to the first four hours after sunset. Fierce little animals, they often prey on things that are bigger than they are. Screech owls are also varied hunters — eating everything from the moths that gather around house lights to crayfish in streams and voles in fields. Contrary to its name, the screech owl's call is melodic and pretty — not at all like a screech.

Screech owls have feather tufts on their heads that look like ears. When the owl is threatened, these tufts bristle, standing on end to make the owl appear taller. Screech owls may also protect themselves through camouflage; stretching and leaning up against a tree, they look like dead branches and are harder to spot. If neither of these defenses work, the owl will squat with its eyes wide open and click its bill like a castanet.

Like all owls, screech owls have twice as many neck bones as humans. This allows them to turn their heads three-quarters of the way around, while humans can only turn their heads one-half of the way.

Glossary

great horned owl: a large owl that preys on rabbits, mice, and smaller owls.

nestling: a baby bird.

pellets: balls of feathers, bones, and other indigestible food parts, which owls cough up.

predator: an animal that hunts and eats other animals.

trill: a wavering song or whistle.